The Rislington Murders

Simply Not Just Cricket

A Murder Mystery Story By Mike Willcox

Simply Not Just Cricket

This is the first in a series of short fictional detective stories set in the 1930s, involving a series of murders in villages throughout the United Kingdom. This initial tale, 'The Rislington Murders (Simply Not Just Cricket)', is set around a local cricket club and involves an extramarital affair and childhood rejection. Although the setting for this murder mystery begins at the local cricket club, the plot thickens when it becomes evident that the bases for all the murders are far from the cricket club.

Author: Mike Willcox
Publisher: Mike Willcox, 2021
First Edition, 2021
Copyright © Mike Willcox, 2021

Proofread by Roy Allen, A-Presto Proofreading Services, Bristol.

Contents

Chapter 1

Cricket Pavilion

It was a hot Wednesday evening in August 1933, and the team captain, John Sims, was picking the cricket team in the cricket pavilion for the following Saturday's match. Felix Mason knocked on the door and asked how the team was looking and whether he would be in next Saturday's match against Morton, who happened to be a very strong cricket team.

John replied, 'Yes, you are in the team on Saturday.'

Felix then asked John, 'Have you heard any of these rumours that Anne Bonn, Tim's wife, is having an affair with one of our players?'

John looked up and very sheepishly said, 'Nope I've not heard anything,' then quickly returned to look at the team sheet he was putting together. Felix added, 'It's just that I've heard some rumours going around about Anne. Still looking down, John added, 'I would not listen to these rumours as they can get out of hand and will cause trouble.'

'Very true, John,' answered Felix. 'Anyway, have you got a full team for Saturday?'

'Yes, I have,' said John, 'but I have to include Josh Parry.'

'Josh Parry?' responded Felix, 'Do you mean that big head who thinks he is our number one player and thinks he should be captain?'

'I know what he thinks, and we all know that he is a third-rate player. However, I have no choice other than to put him in the team as nobody else is available.'

Felix then left soon afterwards, and John waited thirty minutes after that for Felix to arrive home. John then left the pavilion, walked out of the cricket ground and went over to a telephone box. After entering the telephone box, he searched in his pocket for some loose change to ring Anne, hoping that Tim wouldn't answer and that he was out of the house. Anne answered the phone and John asked, 'Are you alone?'

Anne replied, 'Yes, Tim is out walking the dog and will be out for some time.'

'Thank goodness for that!' said John. 'I've just had Felix Mason come into the cricket pavilion while I was picking the team for this coming Saturday when he blurted out that he had heard a rumour that you are having an affair with one of the cricket team.'

'Wow!' answered Anne, 'Who has seen us together, John?'

'I don't know, Anne. We are going to have to be very careful, as I don't want my wife or children to know, let alone your husband.'

'Oh, John my sweetheart, we must be extra careful! I love you so very much and I don't want our relationship to end.'

'Nor do I, my beautiful Anne. See you this coming Friday, as we normally do, my love.'

'Yes, my sweetheart.'

'John, my love, we really must make sure that nobody is following us. I can hear Tim coming up the footpath with our dog, so I must ring off.'

'OK my love, see you Friday.'

John put the phone down and walked back to the cricket pavilion. It was now late in the evening and the sun was going down. The cricket pavilion was in darkness, and as John reached the pavilion, he saw a shadow of a person in the pavilion. He thought, 'Who can that be? I'm sure that I locked the pavilion.' John entered the pavilion and shouted, 'Who is that?' No answer came back, so John walked to the light switch to get some light. However, no lights came on and John heard a movement, so he asked again, 'Who is that and what do you want?'

There was still no answer and everything was very quiet.

Meanwhile, back at John's house, his wife June was wondering where John was as it had started to get late in the evening and John was normally back by 10 o'clock at night. June walked over to the house of one of her sons and asked Jake to go to the cricket club to see if his Dad was OK as he had not come home. June did not ask her other son who still lived at home to go, as father and son had not been getting on very well over the last few days. Jake said, 'Let me get changed into some other clothes, and then I will go and look for dad. You can come with me, mum, if you want, plus it's dark and I would prefer that.'

June agreed and waited for her son to get ready. Ten minutes later, they set off to walk to the cricket ground which was roughly a twenty-minute walk away. When they arrived at the cricket pavilion, the front door was locked and in darkness. Jake banged on the pavilion door and shouted out 'Dad, are you in there?' There was no answer, so Jake got his torch and shone it in through the windows. He couldn't see anything inside except for some paperwork on a table. June told him that it must be the team-sheets for the coming Saturday, which seemed strange as John always put a team-sheet on the notice board and brought one home just in case somebody dropped out so he had to change the team.

Jake asked, 'Where can dad have gone?'

June replied, 'I don't know. We'd better go home just in case your dad is already there.'

They got back to June's house twenty minutes later, but there was no sign of John.

'This is not like your dad, Jake, not without saying he has gone elsewhere.'

'Where is Robert?' asked Jake.

'Oh, I think you'll find him in bed,' responded June.

'Well, he'd better get up as we need to search the village to try and find dad.'

June suggested that they should probably go around to some of the cricket team players just in case he has gone to see one of the team to ask if they were available to play this coming Saturday.

'OK mum, I will get Robert out of bed, and can you find the address book for the players?' Robert was not very pleased about being told to get out of bed to go looking for his dad. His reaction was that dad was sure to turn up soon.

Jake asked him, 'Aren't you worried that dad is out at this time of night?'

Robert's answer was simply, 'Nope.'

'Are going to help me or not?' moaned Jake to which Robert finally agreed, 'If I must, then I will.'

'Well then, get up and get dressed.'

'OK, give a few minutes to put on some clothes.'

Jake went downstairs and asked his mum, 'Have you found the addresses of the cricket team players?'

June answered that she had.

Robert came down ten minutes later. 'OK, let's get out and see if we can find dad,' he said in a grumpy voice.

'Look Robert,' said Jake, 'I know that you and dad don't hit it off much these days, but he is your dad and we need to find him, OK?'

'Yes, I know we need to find him. It's just that it's 12.45 in the morning,' Robert said.

'No, we are not going to be very popular waking people up, but it has got to be done!' replied Jake sharply.

So, off both Jake and Robert went, knocking on the doors of the local team players. After three hours, nobody had seen John by the time they knocked on Felix Mason's door. Felix opened the door very sleepy-eyed, and asked, 'What the heck do you want at this time of the morning?'

'John has not come home and we are out searching for him. Did you see him last night?' 'Jeepers, not come home? Yes, I saw him last night. I went to the cricket pavilion as I knew he was picking the team for this coming Saturday. I left at about 9.30 and he was OK when I left. Have you been to the cricket pavilion?

'Yes, we have, but it's all in darkness and the door is locked, and we don't have a key to get in. Do you?'

'Yes, I do,' answered Felix.

'We shone a torch in through the window and all we could see was some paperwork on a table which we assume to be the sheets for the team.'

'That's unusual for John to leave the team-sheets on the table,' said Felix, 'as he always puts one of them up on the notice board. Let me get dressed and then we can go to the cricket pavilion. Come inside while I get dressed.'

Felix's wife, Faye, shouted down, 'What's wrong?'

Felix shouted back that John Sims had not arrived home yet.

'Oh, dear, what can have happened?'

'We don't know,' responded Felix. 'Anyway my love, we are going to go to the pavilion.'

'OK, I will wait to hear what has happened.'

'Right, let's walk to the cricket pavilion, and if John is not there, we'll need to get hold of the police, June.'

After a twenty-minute walk, they arrived at the pavilion. Felix opened the door and then tried to switch on the lights. When they wouldn't turn on, Felix said, 'That's strange! Have you got your torch, Jake?

'Yes, I have,' replied Jake.

'Let me have it, Jake, and I will go to the fuse box.'

When Felix got to the fuse box, he remarked, 'That's very strange; the fuse box lever is in the off position.' Felix turned the power back on and the lights came on.

'Well, there's no sign of John. Let me check the kitchen. Oh Jesus!'

'What?' June asked anxiously.

'Do not come in here, June!'

'Why? What's wrong?'

Robert followed Felix into the kitchen. 'Oh my God! Dad is on the floor with something tied around his neck and he is not breathing.'

'No, no!' screamed June and she collapsed on the floor.

Jake rushed into the kitchen to see that his dad had been murdered with a ligature around his neck and a crucifix had been placed on top of his body.

'Why, why would anybody want to do this to my dad?'

Felix went to help June who was still in a collapsed state and shouted out, 'Don't touch anything, as we need to get the police.'

June started to recover her composure and asked, 'Why would anybody want to harm my husband?'

'I don't know,' said Jake. 'Look mum, we need to contact the police.'

Robert said, 'I will go to the phone box down the road. Does anybody have any change for the phone?'

Jake said that you don't need any money to ring the police, as it's free to ring 999.

'OK, I'm on my way to the phone box.'

Meanwhile, Felix and Jake comforted June until a policeman arrived. When the local police constable did arrive, they showed him John's body, then explained what had happened and how they came to find him there in the pavilion. The policeman asked if they had touched anything which they denied, other than the fuse box which had been turned off. The policeman then said that this was a job for the CID (the Criminal Investigation Department) which they didn't have in the village of Rislington.

'I will have to contact the police in the town of Oakley and I can only do this from my police house.'

'What is your name, Constable?' asked Jake. 'My name is Colin Denstun,' answered the policeman.

Jake added, 'I only asked so I know who we are dealing with.'

PC Denstun then asked for the keys of the pavilion and also asked who else had got those keys.

Felix responded that only he and John had keys to the pavilion, as John was the captain of the cricket club and he was the vice-captain.

'I don't know whether the keys are on John's body, but the pavilion was locked when we came to look for John, so I don't know whether the person who has done this to John has now got the keys.'

PC Denstun told them, 'You all need to go home now. I know it's difficult for you, but I have to lock up here as it is now a crime scene.'

Felix said, 'I will walk home with you and the boys, June.'

'Thank you,' responded the tearful June.

Chapter 2

Crime Scene

PC Denstun contacted Oakley police, and Detective Chief Inspector Dave Jackson and his assistant, Tom Bellson, arrived at the crime scene shortly afterwards. PC Denstun had stayed there to meet them. Jackson and Bellson looked at the body and could see the ligature around the neck of the victim's body as well as the crucifix that had been placed on his chest. Jackson wondered aloud, 'Now, why would anybody want to put a crucifix on top of the body of a person they had just murdered?'

Bellson asked Denstun if there had been any sign of the forensic guy. Denstun replied that he'd seen him driving into the cricket ground.

'Great,' said Bellson, just as Tony Johnson, the forensic scientist, walked into the pavilion. Tony said, 'I hear you have a dead body for me to investigate.'

'Yes,' replied Jackson, 'it's out the back in the kitchen.'

Tony walked into the kitchen. 'Wow!' he said, 'I've not seen a death like this before. The ligature is still tied tightly around his neck, and it looks like there's some sort of toggle to stop it from releasing. I can't see any other marks on the body at the moment, but I will need to take the body away for a further examination.'

Bellson responded, 'We know that the fuse box was switched off as the lights did not work when his body was found and I was told that Felix Mason switched the fuse box back on. This means that you will find his fingerprints on the lever.'

'OK Dave, I will need his fingerprints plus those of all the family who found the body. Can we now take photos and dust for prints, so that the body can be moved to the forensic lab? I see there is a crucifix on the body. Do you know anything about that, Dave?

'Nope,' responded Dave, 'it was there when the body was found. I will test for fingerprints, although I don't know if there will be any.'

Jackson asked how long it would be before they took the body away and Tony responded that he would arrange for the body to be moved as soon as he had finished, which would be in about two hours' time. Jackson and Bellson left while PC Denstun continued to stay at the crime scene.

Jackson told Bellson, 'We need all the names and addresses of everybody who has anything to do with the cricket club. I suggest that you try Felix Mason and I will go and see the deceased man's wife.'

When DCI Jackson arrived at John Sims' house, Jake answered the door and invited him in to the front room where his mother was sitting. Jackson explained, 'Sorry to have to ask these questions at a time like this, but I have to do this.'

Jake said that he understood. 'Mrs Sims, what time did your husband leave last night to go to the cricket pavilion?'

'My husband left at about 7.15 pm.'

'What time did you expect your husband to be home?' asked Jackson.

June replied that he was always home by 10 pm, which is why she was worried when he hadn't come home. Jackson asked what she did next, to which June replied, 'My sons and I walked to the cricket ground and looked as best as we could inside the pavilion with a torch through the windows, as I don't have the keys to the pavilion. We could see some paperwork on a table which I assumed was the pile of team-sheets for this weekend's cricket match.'

Jackson asked what happened next and June replied, 'We then went to Felix Mason's house when he told us that he had also been to the cricket pavilion and had left the pavilion at about 9.30 pm. Anyway, Felix had a set of keys and he came with us to the pavilion and that's when we found my husband, John, on the floor of the kitchen and you now know the rest of what happened.'

Jackson then asked, 'Do you know why anybody would want to do this to your husband?'

'No I don't,' sobbed June.

'How has your husband been lately?' asked Jackson. 'What I mean is, has his attitude changed at all recently?'

'Not at all,' replied June.

'How about your sons? How did they get on with their father?'

'Well, Jake gets, sorry, got on very well with his dad and he lives with his wife. Robert, who lives here at home, doesn't always hit it off with him, as they had what you might say a love-hate relationship. They were always arguing. John has always said that Robert can never do anything right.'

'OK, Mrs Sims, that's all I need for now. I will contact you soon when I have more information about the case or if I need more information from you or your sons. Oh, before I go, the cricket match this coming weekend will need to be cancelled as the cricket pavilion is now a crime scene.'

'You will need to speak to Felix Mason as he is the vice-captain,' advised June.

'Thanks for that,' Jackson said before he left.

Back at the police house, Bellson and PC Denstun were sitting down, each having a cup of tea when DCI Jackson arrived.

'Ah, that is just what I need, said Jackson. 'Is there any tea left in the pot, Denstun?'

'Yes there is,' replied Denstun.

'Can you pour another cup for me then, please? Now then, we need to have the cricket match due this weekend cancelled.'

'That's already been done, Sir. Felix Mason has cancelled it.'

'Brilliant,' said Jackson, 'Bellson, did you take a statement from Mason on what happened last night?'

'I did,' replied Bellson, 'and something significant was said by Mason to the deceased.' 'What was that?' asked Jackson.

'Well, there is a rumour going around that one of the cricketer's wives is having an affair with another cricketer from the team and Mason told the deceased John Sims who tried to ignore it and just told Mason not to listen to gossip.'

Jackson asked, 'Does he know who the woman is?'

'Yes, he does. She is the wife of Tim Bonn and her name is Anne. He also said that she is a bit of a flirt when men are around her, which I gather does annoy her husband.'

Jackson responded, 'I think any husband would feel the same and if this is true about an affair, could it be that she was seeing John Sims? We need to go and talk to this Anne Bonn. We will need a female PC with us, because if there is any truth in this allegation, we may have an upsetting scene, and as we don't have a female PC here in Rislington, we need one to come from Oakley and we need her here today. In fact, Bellson, take my car and fetch a PC now. I will ring the Oakley station to organise that straightaway. We will wait here in the police house until you get back.

Two hours later, Bellson arrived back with PC Sue Brittan, where they found DCI Jackson waiting for them.

'Have you informed PC Brittan what is this all about and why we need her?' he asked.

'I have,' replied Bellson.

'Right, here's the address, Bellson. Let's go and see Anne Bonn's reaction when we speak to her.'

On arrival, Jackson remarked, 'Wow! This is a house and a half; somebody has got some money.'

Bellson explained, 'Felix Mason told me that her husband is a business man and spends a lot of time away on business.'

'Well,' said Jackson, 'he is going to be in shock if these rumours are true.'

Bellson knocked on the door, introduced himself to the lady who opened it and asked, 'Are you Anne Bonn?'

'Yes, I am. Why?' she responded.

'We need to come inside to speak to you.'

After letting them in, Anne asked, 'Has something happened to my husband?'

'This is not about your husband. Do you know John Sims?'

'Well, yes I do,' answered Anne. 'He plays cricket with my husband Tim who is away on business at the moment. Why?'

Jackson continued, 'The reason we are here is that John Sims was found dead last night at the cricket pavilion.'

On hearing that, Anne screamed out, 'No, no, no!' and burst into tears, collapsing onto the settee. Jackson asked how well she knew John Sims. Still crying, she queried, 'Why do you ask that question?'

'Why do I ask that question? It's because we've been told that you were having an affair with one of the cricket team. We need to know if it was John Sims and if it was, we need to know the truth right now, because we will find out sooner or later, and this will stop a lot of heartache in the future. So, were you having an affair with John Sims?'

Sobbing her eyes out, Anne answered, 'Yes, I was.'

Jackson asked, 'Who else knows about this affair?'

'I didn't think anybody knew about it, although last night, John rang me at about 10 pm saying Felix had told him that a rumour was going around that I was having an affair with somebody from the cricket club, so we were going to meet this Friday like we always do and talk about it.'

'So, your husband does not know?' asked Jackson.

Anne replied, 'No, and neither does my son, as far as I'm aware.'

Jackson asked, 'How old is your son and does he still live at home?'

'My son is 22 and yes, he lives here with us. Why do you want to know?'

'It's just part of the investigation', replied Jackson. 'I need to know everything when dealing with a murder. You say that your husband is away on business. Where is that? Is he still in the UK?'

'I'm not sure exactly where, but it's somewhere in the north of England, yes. Tim is on the move all the time selling various products to shops.'

'OK, that's all for now, but I will need to speak to your husband when he gets back home.'

'Well, he should be home at some point tomorrow afternoon,' replied Anne as they left.

Once back at the police house, Jackson and Bellson began to try to piece together what had happened and discussed the suspects who could have committed the murder of John Sims.

'Well,' said Bellson, 'I see five family members who would be upset at this relationship if they knew about it. These are Tim Bonn and his son, the deceased's sons, Jake and Robert, and of course, the deceased's wife, June.'

Jackson commented, 'What about the rumour that Felix Mason heard about this affair. Did Mason give you any indication about where he heard this?'

'Yes, he did. It was just general talk at the local pub, although Mason doesn't know how or where the rumour started.'

'Thanks, but that's not much help, Bellson. I can see that we are going around in circles. The question is, "Did Tim Bonn know about this relationship between his wife and John Sims?" We know that Anne Bonn is a flirt with men and he did not approve. Even though his wife said that he was away on business doesn't necessarily mean that he didn't come back on Wednesday night to murder John Sims, then went back to wherever he had been on business. So, we need to talk to both Tim Bonn and his son. Do you know his son's name, Bellson?'

'I'm told it is Paul,' answered Bellson.

The telephone rang and Jackson answered. It was Tony from forensics and, when asked if there was anything new to add to what they already knew, he explained what he had managed to find.

'Really?' asked Jackson, 'So Sims was hit on the head, but there was no blood so you're saying that it was just hard enough to knock him out, and then the ligature was put around his neck. Were there any fingerprints on the crucifix?'

'There were no fingerprints.'

'The killer must have used gloves by the sound of it which is of no help to us. So, I guess there were no other prints then?'

Tony answered that there were too many fingerprints which would belong to all the cricket players and that there were no keys on the body, adding, 'So, whoever did it has taken the pavilion keys and regarding what hit the deceased, I would say that it was a round piece of wood like a rounders bat or something similar to that.'

'OK,' responded Jackson, 'thanks for that and can you let me have your report as soon as possible?'

Chapter 3

Collating Evidence

It was Friday afternoon and Tim Bonn walked into the police house where Jackson and Bellson were waiting for him.

'Come in, Mr Bonn, and take a seat. We will be with you soon.'

Jackson and Bellson joined him five minutes later. Tim Bonn asked, 'Why do you need to see me as I only found a note at home when I came in? My wife is out at the moment so I don't know why you wish to see me.'

Jackson replied, 'So, you haven't heard that John Sims was murdered last Wednesday then?'

'What? You're not serious?' shouted out a shocked-looking Tim Bonn.

'I'm afraid so. He was found murdered in the cricket club pavilion,' explained Jackson, 'and I think that the reason I need to speak to you might be quite painful for you, as we had information that there was something going on between your wife and John Sims.'

'What do you mean, "something going on"?' asked Bonn quizzically.

'Well,' responded Jackson, 'there has been a rumour that your wife and Sims had been having an affair and your wife has since confirmed this to us.'

'Blimey! I knew my wife can flirt with men which does cause arguments between us, but to have an affair is a real shock, and I find this very hard to understand. I'll need to talk to my wife.'

Jackson then asked, 'I hear that you have been away on business. Where have you been as we need to know where you were on Wednesday evening?'

'I have been in Yorkshire since Monday and came back today. I stayed in the same bed and breakfast lodgings, so on Wednesday evening, I had a meal in a restaurant, and then went to the lodgings which I always use when I am in Yorkshire.'

Jackson explained that he will need proof such as receipts and the address and telephone number of his lodgings.

'I can do that,' replied Bonn, 'but I will need them back otherwise I cannot claim my expenses. I can let you have them tomorrow morning.'

'Yes, that will be fine. Give them to PC Denstun, and when we've finished with them, you can have them back.' Tim Bonn was allowed to leave soon after that.

'Right, Bellson, I need to go and see Mrs Sims and her two sons,' Jackson said, before getting in his car and driving to the Sims' house.

After arriving, Jackson knocked on the door which Robert, the younger son, answered.

'Is your mother in?' asked Jackson.

'Yes, she is. You'd better come in.'

Robert then showed Jackson into the front room and Mrs Sims soon followed Jackson into the room.

'Mrs Sims, I need to ask you some more questions and also your sons as well, so Robert, I need you to sit with us. Now, I need to know what you were doing on Wednesday night before you went looking for your husband.'

Mrs Sims answered, 'I was sat at home reading a book which I do most evenings.'

'What about you, Robert?' asked Jackson.

Robert answered, 'I went out at about 6.30 to visit a friend's house and then came back home at about 9.30. I went to my bedroom and stayed there until mum became worried about dad after which when we went searching for him and you know what happened after that.'

'That's fine,' said Jackson. 'I will need to know your friend's name and address, so I can verify this. Now, Mrs Sims, I'm sorry to have to ask this, but was your marriage OK?'

'What do you mean by that?' asked June abruptly.

'Well, Mrs Sims, we learnt from Felix Mason that there was a rumour going around that Anne Bonn, the wife of Tim Bonn, was having an affair with one of the cricketers and it appears that it was your husband. Anne Bonn has confirmed that she has been seeing your husband on Friday nights.'

'Oh my God,' shouted June, 'this can't be true!'

Robert piped in to say, 'I saw dad on a Friday night the other week getting off the local bus with a woman. I wouldn't know this Bonn woman as I don't have anything to do with the cricket club.'

Jackson asked which bus this was.

'It was the number 10 bus, which goes to all the local villages around here, so if dad was seeing this woman, they must have been going to another village where they wouldn't be recognised.'

June Sims looking shocked. 'I don't understand why John would want to see someone. I thought everything was OK with us, and regarding Friday evening, John always told me that he went to the pub as he enjoyed a glass of ale. Before you ask, I don't drink, so I never go the pub.'

Just as Jackson was leaving, he asked, 'Can you tell your other son that I need to speak to him and if possible, tomorrow at the local police house?'

On Saturday morning, Anne Bonn's son, Paul, visited the police house and PC Denstun took him into the interview room, telling him to wait there until the inspectors arrived from Oakley. Fifteen minutes later, Jackson arrived with Bellson. PC Denstun informed Jackson that Paul Bonn was in the interview room.

'OK,' said Jackson, 'I will see him now.'

On walking into the room he spoke with the young lad, 'I trust you know why you are here Mr Bonn.'

'Yes, I do. My father has told me what's happened and also about my mother. Why do you want to see me?'

'Well, the reason we need to talk to you is, first of all, we don't know if John Sims' murder is connected to his relationship with your mother and, if it is, then we have to check out all the avenues, so we need to know what you were doing last Wednesday evening.'

'That's easy. I spent the evening at home in my bedroom listening to the radio which is what I do every Wednesday night. My mum should be able to verify that as she was downstairs in the backroom.'

'OK that's all for now. If we need any more information, we will contact you again. Bellson, please see Mr Bonn out.'

Ten minutes later, Jake Sims arrived and was taken into the interview room.

'OK, Mr Sims, have you been told by your mother what we spoke about last night?' asked Jackson.

'Yes, she told me this morning, and as for Anne Bonn, I knew she was a flirt with the male cricketers and I've seen her make a pass at my dad, but he always seemed to laugh at her so I found this hard to believe.'

'Well, Mr Sims, Anne Bonn has confirmed that they had been seeing each other on Friday nights and I have said to everybody else that we don't know at the moment whether this is connected to the murder of your father. Now, what I need to know from you are your movements on Wednesday night.'

Jake replied, 'I arrived home from work at 6 pm, then sat down and had my evening meal with my wife. After that, I spent the rest of the evening listening to the radio with my wife until my mum arrived at the door saying that dad had not come home from the cricket club, and the rest you know.'

'OK, Mr Sims, that is all I require from you for the moment,' and, after that, Jake Sims left the police house.

Jackson and Bellson sat down to collate all of the evidence they had gathered so far and drove back to Oakley after telling PC Denstun that they would be back on the following Monday morning unless something cropped up in the meantime. 'In that case, just ring the Oakley Police Station,' instructed Jackson.

Chapter 4

The Mystery Deepens

On the following Sunday evening, another member of the Rislington cricket club, Simon Rush, who was retired and lived next door to Anne Bonn, took his usual evening walk with Ben, his Labrador retriever dog. Leaving the house at about 7.30, he said to his wife, Jane, 'I will be back about 8.30.'

As he walked up the garden path and opened his front gate, Anne Bonn shouted out, 'Have you heard about John Sims?'
'Yes, I have, and it is a dreadful business; he was such a good friend and a very good cricket player who did so much for the club. Simon Rush shut the front gate and walked towards the countryside, passing the last house in the village at about 7.50 when he shouted, 'Hello' to Andy Tub who was tidying up his front garden. He then carried on walking with his dog out into the countryside where Ben could be let off the lead.

A while later, back at Simon Rush's house, his wife was starting to worry as the time had reached 9 pm and Simon had not come back home from his walk with Ben. At that moment, Jane heard a bark at the front door and, when she opened the door, she could only see Ben by himself and Simon was nowhere to be seen. Jane walked up the path to look for Simon, then knocked on her neighbours' doors to see if he had popped in to see of them, which he hadn't.

'Where can my husband be?' asked Jane to her neighbour, Steve, 'This is not like Simon at all.'

Steve asked, 'Do you know where Simon walks with your dog?'

'Yes, I think so.'

'OK, let me put a jacket on and we'd better go and look for Simon.'

Jane and Steve left soon afterwards and followed the route that Jane was sure which Simon usually took with Ben. As they were walking past Andy Tub's house, he was still in his garden, and Jane asked Andy if Simon had gone past his house that night.

'Yes,' answered Andy, 'although I haven't seen Simon come back yet. Why do you ask?'

Jane told him that their dog, Ben, had come home by himself and there was no sign of Simon. It was now getting late and dark.

'Well, Jane, it is going to get much darker now as from here it is countryside and no lights. Have you got a torch?'

'No, we don't have a torch.'

'OK Jane, I have one, so I will go into my house and I will come with you.'

'Thank you, Andy,' answered Jane. Soon afterwards, all three of them started walking into the countryside and began shouting Simon's name, yet it was to no avail.

Andy told Jane and Steve, 'This is like looking for a needle in a haystack. We have fields on both sides and then woodland. Simon could be anywhere.'

Jane asked, 'Can you remember what time Simon went past your house tonight, as Simon left home at 7.30 and he would normally be back by about 8.30?'

'I think it was about 7.50, Jane, so on that basis, Simon would have only walked about ten more minutes past your house and we have walked further than that now.'

'God knows where Simon is!' screamed Jane. 'What has happened to my husband?'

'Jane, I think we'd better contact the police as we need more help to find Simon.'

'I agree, Jane,' said Andy, 'and then they can get a search party out, otherwise we could be here all night and still not find Simon. However, before we do that, we need to go back to your house just in case he has gone back home.'

They walked back to Jane's house. When they arrived, there were no lights on. After Jane had opened the front door, she shouted Simon's name, but there was no answer.

'Simon has not come back home. Right then, it is time to visit the police.'

All three walked to the police house and Jane pressed the police bell at the entrance. PC Denstun opened the door and asked what the problem was.

Jane explained that her husband Simon had gone missing after taking their dog, Ben, out for a walk and that they had been out looking for Simon and couldn't find him.

'It's now 11.15 at night and Simon should have been home by about 8.30,' added a worried Jane.

'You'd better come in and tell me which route your husband took with your dog and what type of dog is with your husband.'

Jane explained that the route Simon took was along Shipley Lane then out into the countryside and she knew that Simon past Andy's house at about 7.50 which is the last house in Shipley Lane before going into the countryside which is fields and woodland.

She finished by saying, 'The dog came home by himself, so God knows where my husband is.'

'Please let me know your name,' asked PC Denstun.

'My name is Jane Rush. What happens now?'

PC Denstun explained, 'I can't do anything at this time of night, as it is pitch black out in the countryside, so that is too dangerous even with a search party. I am afraid that we will have to wait until tomorrow morning. I will contact Oakley Police Station to get more help out here so we can search for your husband. In the meantime, please go back home and get some rest, and if your husband does show up, then contact me straight away. I am sure your husband will be OK.' On that note, Steve walked Jane home.

The following day, Dave Jackson and Tom Bellson arrived at the police house and PC Denstun briefed them on what had happened the previous night. Jackson then rang Oakley Police Station to ask for a search party to come to Rislington. Jane arrived at the police house and Jackson spoke with her immediately, 'I presume your husband has not come back.'

'No, he hasn't. I just don't understand what has happened.'

Jackson then explained that a group of police officers were coming from Oakley to search for her husband.

He continued, 'Now, PC Denstun has told us where your husband went, so my advice is for you to go home and we will contact you as soon as we know anything.'

'Can I not come with you, please?' pleaded Jane.

'I'd rather you didn't, Mrs Rush. Our police officers do know what they are doing and, as I said, we will contact as soon as we find your husband.'

Two hours later, Police Sergeant Combes arrived in a police van with eleven constables. DCI Jackson gave Sergeant Combes instructions about where to search for Simon Rush, starting at the end of Shipley Lane. Sergeant Combes drove the constables down Shipley Lane, followed by Jackson and Bellson, and they parked their vehicles at the end of the road. Combes ordered his men to search the two fields either side of the road before searching the woods. After an hour, Simon Rush was still not found, so they started their search in the woods on the left-hand side of the road which was full of pathways and was less densely populated with trees than the other side of the road. After another hour, there was still no sign of Simon Rush, when one of the constables suddenly blew his whistle. Jackson and Bellson made their way to the constable whereupon they saw a body lying face down on the pathway between some bushes.

Jackson shouted to Sergeant Combes, 'We need forensics from Oakley and that should include Tony Collins.'

Combes drove back to the police house to ring Tony Collins. Meanwhile, Jackson started to look over the body to discover a ligature around the body and neck just the same as John Sims had around his neck plus some blood on the back of his head. He then noticed that there was a crucifix lying on the ground next to the body.

'This is an identical murder to that of John Sims,' Jackson told Bellson.

'Now, what is the connection? Is it Anne Bonn or is it anything to do with the cricket club as they both played cricket for the Rislington club?'

'Good question,' replied Bellson.

'Ah, here come the forensics! Tony, it looks like we have the same M O as John Sims.'

'Nasty,' said Tony, 'and I can see this time that the blow to the head caused bleeding. I see we have a crucifix again and, judging by the state of the body, he has been dead for ten or more hours.'

Bellson explained that he had been missing since the previous night after taking his dog for a walk. He added, 'We will need to have the body identified by his wife.'

'That's fine. I will have the body moved later this morning, do a detailed analysis for my report on the death, and then you can do the identification of the body which can be done tomorrow morning,' answered Tony.

'Right, Bellson, we need to go and see Jane Rush to give her the news of her husband,' sighed Jackson.

They arrived at Jane Rush's house and knocked on the door. Jane opened the door and asked, 'Have you found my husband and is he alright?'

'Mrs Rush, can we come in please, as we have some bad news for you?'

'Dear God, what's happened?' pleaded Jane.

Jackson explained, 'We have found a body in the woods which we believe to be your husband, I am sorry to say.'

Jane collapsed into a chair screaming, 'No, no, this can't be true!'

'Bellson, go and make Mrs Rush a cup of sweet tea. Now, Mrs Rush, we will need you to identify your husband's body tomorrow morning. We will send a police car to pick you up at around 10.30 am.'

'Can I not see my husband today?' asked Jane.

'I'm afraid not, Mrs Rush, as forensics have to establish what happened to your husband before you can see him.'

'How did it happen?' Jane asked.

'I cannot give any details at the moment, at least until the forensics have finished their examination and we can start our investigation into the death of your husband,' explained Jackson. 'Do you have anybody who can stay with you, Mrs Rush?' he asked her.

'Not really, as I don't have any other family. What I will do is speak to Steve next door as we are good friends. When you leave, I will go and see Steve and his wife.'

Back at the police house, Jackson was speaking to Bellson about two Rislington cricket players being murdered and both in the same way.

'We now need to interview all the cricket club members to see if we can get to the bottom of this, and the other thing which is foxing me is why crucifixes are being left with the bodies and does the local church have anything to do with these deaths? I wonder if Rush and Sims ever frequented the local church. I will need to speak to the vicar, and do we have all the names and addresses of the cricket club members?'

'Yes we do,' answered Bellson. 'PC Denstun has got them.'

'Right then, tomorrow's task is to start interviewing them all.'

The time was 4.40 pm, so Jackson and Bellson drove back to Oakley Police Station.

Jane Rush arrived at the mortuary the following day and Jackson accompanied Jane to identify the body. Jane tearfully confirmed that it was her husband, so Jackson took Jane back to the Oakley Police Station to ask questions about her husband.

'I'm sorry to have to speak to you now about your husband, but I have to start somewhere in the investigation. Now, I have to inform you that your husband and John Sims were both murdered in the same way and I'm unsure of what the connection is at the moment other than that they both played for the Rislington cricket club. Now, did your husband socialise with John Sims outside of the cricket club?

Jane answered, 'No they didn't; the only time they were together was when they were playing cricket on a Saturday, so what the connection is, I just don't know.'

'Now, I have to ask you a delicate question about your marriage. Was your marriage fine?'

'Yes, it was. Why do you ask?'

'The reason I ask is because John Sims and your next-door neighbour, Anne Bonn, had been seeing each other.'

35

'That's news to me,' Jane said. 'I know she is a flirt with the men and has even flirted with Simon which we took as a joke and just brushed it off. However, regarding, Anne and John, are you sure?'

Jackson replied that Anne Bonn had already confirmed that she was seeing John Sims.

'Goodness me,' said Jane, 'I never knew that.'

'Now you see why I was asking that question about you and your husband.'

'Yes, I understand that now, but myself and Simon always did everything together. I even went to the cricket matches and helped with the teas.'

'Thank you for that, Mrs Rush. I will get someone to take you back home and will contact you when I know more or if I need more information from you.'

Jackson then walked back to the police station and, as he entered the building, Bellson told him, 'The forensic report on Simon Rush is on your desk.'

Jackson read the report, and remarked, 'As I suspected, Rush was murdered in the same way as Sims. The only difference was when he was hit on the head, bleeding was caused on Rush's head, yet not on Sims head, and again no fingerprints were found, so whoever did this is using gloves. Bellson, we now need to interview all of the members of the Rislington cricket team as the connection to these murders must be something to do with this club, but I don't know what at the moment. I will start with Felix Mason today, as I wish to know where and when he heard these rumours about Sims and Mrs Bonn. Bellson, you can start with Paul Way.'

'Will do, but I will have to wait until this evening, as Way and most of the cricket team will be at work.'

'That's true, Bellson. I will go and see Felix Mason tonight.'

Later that day, during the evening, DCI Jackson knocked on Felix Mason's door and was invited into the front room.

'Mr Mason, I require some more information from you regarding the rumours you heard about Anne Bonn having an affair with one of the cricket team. Where did you hear this and who did you hear say it?

Felix replied, 'I heard it the night before John Sims was murdered in the Rislington Arms pub. A few of us from the cricket club usually meet on a Tuesday evening for a social drink and, while chatting away, someone said, "Have you heard about these rumours about Anne Bonn having an affair?" I can't remember who said it now; we just brushed it off as we all know she likes to flirt with the men. The problem with Anne is that Tim is always away on business most of the week, so Anne gets bored of being on her own.'

Jackson asked, 'Does Anne Bonn ever join you at the pub on Tuesday evenings?'

'Yes, she does join us on some evenings, although not last Tuesday.'

'What about John Sims?' asked Jackson.

'Only on very rare occasions; in fact, I can't remember the last time John joined us as he used to spend most of his time at the cricket ground.'

Jackson then told him, 'I will need the names of all the cricket members who were with you last Tuesday.'

'From what I can remember, the names you want are Jason Pullman, Tom Butch, Ron Cotter, Andy Tub and I think Josh Parry was there as well.'

'Thanks for that. We will need to speak to these cricketers in the next few days.'

The following day, Jackson and Bellson were discussing the case at Oakley Police Station.

Bellson asked, 'How did it go with Paul Way?'

'According to Paul Way, he was home all night with his wife which she confirmed. I also went and spoke to Jason Pullman and, again, he was at home with his wife, so no joy with either of them.'

'How about Felix Mason?' asked Bellson.

Jackson replied that these rumours were heard the night before Sims was murdered in the pub and a few of the cricket team were there.'

'Who said that about Sims and Bonn though?'

'He can't remember now. Whether that is the truth is another question.'

'I think you'll need to speak to the rest of the cricket team,' decided Jackson. 'Can you do that today, Bellson?'

'I can,' replied Bellson.

'I need to speak to the local vicar today and Anne Bonn again,' said Jackson, before he walked out of the police station, jumped into his car and drove to the Rislington church in Saint Jude's. He knocked on the rectory door, and when the vicar's wife opened it, he asked, 'Is the vicar in, as I wish to speak to him?'

'My husband is in the church vestry. If you walk into the church and shout "Tom", he will hear you and then come out to see you.'

'Thank you,' said Jackson, who then walked to the church, entered through the main door of the church, and shouted, 'Tom!'

The vicar came out and asked if could be of any help.

'Yes please,' replied Jackson, 'I am DCI Dave Jackson, investigating the murders of John Sims and Simon Rush.'

'Oh, it's such a dreadful business,' the vicar replied, 'and how can I help you?'

'Well, when we found the dead bodies, they each had a crucifix laid on top of them and we don't know what the significance of this is at the moment. What we are wondering is if it is anything to do with the church. I have one of the crucifixes with me. Have you seen one like this before and do you have these in your church?'

The vicar looked at the crucifix.

'I've never seen one like this before,' he said. 'The only crucifixes we give out are on Palm Sunday and those are made of dried palm leaves, so sorry I cannot help you.'

'Can I just ask one more question?' asked Jackson. 'Do any of the cricket team come to your church?'

'Yes, they do,' replied the vicar. 'In fact, I sometimes play for them if they are short of a player. I'm not a very good player, but as I said, if they don't have a full team, I play for them. I also go and watch them play on a Saturday afternoon quite often.'

'Thank you for your time, vicar,' said Jackson, and after leaving the church, he drove to Anne Bonn's house. Soon after he had knocked, Anne opened it and invited Jackson into the front room where they both sat down. Jackson then asked Anne, 'I am trying to see if there is any connection between you and Simon Rush, as his wife says nothing has ever happened between you and Simon.'

'Ah,' said Anne, 'before I met Tim, I went out with Simon for six months which is a long time ago. Simon and I both come from the next village, Brunton.'

'Really?' said Jackson. 'Now that gives me a link between Rush and Sims. Do you ever go back to Brunton village?'

'Yes,' replied Anne, 'that is where John and myself went every Friday night and spent the evening in the pub in Brunton. They have a private room where we could be together secretly. I know the landlord as he is an old friend of my family.'

Jackson asked what the name of the pub was.

'It's called "The Hollybush",' replied Anne.

Jackson asked, 'Do any of the Rislington Cricket team frequent The Hollybush pub?'

'Not to my knowledge,' replied Anne, 'and that is why we used to go there.'

Jackson left Anne Bonn's house and drove back to Oakley Police Station to find Bellson already back at the station. He gave all his new information to Bellson, and stated, 'We finally have a link between Sims and Rush. How did you get on today, Bellson?'

Bellson responded, 'I've interviewed all the other players who all have alibis for when Sims was murdered, apart from one called Josh Parry. He owns the shoe shop in the high street. He shut the shop at midday as it was half-day closing that day. He has two staff members who he sent home while he waited for the delivery of new stock. That arrived at about 2 pm and I've seen the paperwork confirming the delivery. He then redressed the front window with the new stock which he says took him until about 4.30 pm, after which he went to his back office to do his accounts for the previous week's takings, finally leaving the shop at around 7 pm when he went home, had a meal, sat down and relaxed for the rest of the evening. I asked him if he was on his own and he replied, "Yes, I am single and have never been married." When I asked him if anyone could verify his movements, he responded, "I haven't spoken to anybody since midday other than the delivery man with the new stock", so I don't think so, no.'

'OK Bellson, it's getting late now,' remarked Jackson. 'We will call it a day for now as it's time to go home and get something to eat.'

Chapter 5

All Very Sinister and Treacherous

Two days later, DCI Jackson revisited June Sims. 'I need to ask you some questions about your sons, Robert and Jake, and their relationship with their father,' he said. 'Now, I believe Robert and his father didn't see eye-to-eye.'

'Yes, that is true,' replied June.

'I need to know why this was,' asked Jackson.

'You see,' explained June, 'my younger son, Robert, spends a lot of time with an older man and doesn't seem interested in females, which my husband said was very unhealthy and I must admit that I feel the same although I don't say anything as I wish to keep the piece in the household. There were always so many rows between my husband and Robert that I would often cry trying to stop them arguing.'

Jackson then stated, 'I understand that Robert saw your husband getting off the local bus with a woman on a Friday night about three or four weeks ago.'

'Yes,' said June, 'I learnt this after John's death. I always thought John was at the cricket club as he spent so much time there.'

'Well, I regret to tell you, Mrs Sims, that your husband was seeing Anne Bonn every Friday night and they would catch the bus to the village of Brunton and spend the evening in the Hollybush pub.'

'So, it's true what I've been hearing in our village about my husband and Anne Bonn! I am finding this very hard to understand as I always thought our marriage was a sound one. Do you know how long this had been going on?'

'I'm afraid I don't,' answered Jackson. 'Now, I will need to speak to Robert.'

'Why?' asked June. 'You don't suspect Robert did this to my husband, do you?'

Jackson explained, 'At the moment everybody is a suspect, and for now, I have to follow every avenue and your son certainly had a motive with the way things were between them.'

At that very moment, Robert walked in through the front door. June called Robert to come into the front room.

Once he had entered, his Mum told him, 'DCI Jackson wants to talk to you about your relationship with your dad. I've told him about the arguments you were having with your dad regarding your spending time with an older man.'

Robert shouted, 'Why do you want to know that? I do what I want in my private life which is exactly what I always told my dad!'

'Look Robert, I am trying to find out who murdered your father and I have to look at every angle and everybody is a suspect, including you, especially as I know things were not good between the two of you. So, I need to know your movements on the Friday night, the 12th of August.'

'I've already told you that before!' shouted Robert.

'Calm down, Robert. I just want you to repeat what you said before.'

'OK,' said Robert, 'I visited a friend of mine, then came home at about 9 pm and went straight to my room and stayed there until Jake got me out of bed to go out and find my dad which did not please me at the time.'

Jackson asked, 'Did you hear Robert come in, Mrs Sims?

'To be honest, I can't remember.'

'Mum,' shouted Robert, 'surely you heard me come in!'

'Look Robert, my head is so jumbled up with what is happening.'

'We will leave it at that for the moment, but what I need is the name and address of who you saw that evening, Robert.'

'No way!' retorted Robert back at Jackson. 'That is my private life and no one interferes with that, not even the police.'

'I'm sorry,' said Jackson, 'I have to know. This is a murder investigation, Robert, so who is the person you spent the evening with?'

'I'm worried that this this will become public information and I don't want that to happen.'

'Look Robert, this will not be public information, nor will the press know,' promised Jackson.

'OK,' said Robert, 'his name Shane Dobbs and he lives at Fish House, The Avenue, Rislington.'

'Now, I also have Jake's address, so I will interview him at his home,' said Jackson before he left to drive straight to Jake's address.

Jake was in his front garden. 'Hello Jake, I need to tie up a few loose ends.'

Jake invited DCI Jackson into his house. 'How can I help you?'

'Well firstly, all I can confirm is that your father was in a relationship with Anne Bonn and that every Friday night, they would travel by bus to the next village of Brunton and spend the evening in the Hollybush pub.'

'Oh dear me, what on earth did my father gain from that? Mum and dad always seemed to have a happy relationship. I just don't understand.'

'I have to ask you, Jake, about your relationship with your father.

Jake replied, 'We always got on very well together. It's just my brother who didn't hit it off with dad.'

'Yes, I know,' explained Jackson, 'I have just been talking to Robert and he has told me why.'

'How do you feel about your brother's relationship with this man he's seeing?'

Jake replied, 'I just ignore it; there's just too much hassle and it causes rows within the family, especially with dad.'

'Thanks for that. Jake. By the way, do you know Shane Dobbs?'

'Not really. I have seen him in the street, but have never spoken to him.'

Jackson left Jake's house and drove straight to Shane Dobbs' cottage, where he was out in his front garden.

Jackson asked, 'Are you Shane Dobbs?'

'Yes, I am,' replied Shane, 'and what do you want?'

'I am DCI Jackson, investigating the murder of John Sims. I believe that his son, Robert, is friends with you.'

'Yes, we are friends and how can I help you?'

45

Jackson asked, 'On the night of John Sims' death, did Robert Sims spend any time with you, and if so, what time did he go home?'

'Yes, Robert was here with me. We like to listen to music together and if I remember rightly, Robert left here at about 9 pm to go home as he needed to be up early the next morning to go to work.'

'That's all I needed to know, thank you, Mr Dobbs.'

Jackson drove back to Oakley Police Station and called Bellson into his office to discuss the case.

'We just seem to be going around in circles and the only link we have at the moment is that Anne Bonn is at the centre of the link. It's got to be something about relationships with Anne Bonn. Is it someone she has rejected, and if so, who and why? What about the crucifixes left on top of the two bodies? They obviously have some meaning, but even the local vicar could not give me any reason when I spoke with him. It's now late in the evening, so it's time to go home. We can go through all the evidence again tomorrow, as there must be something staring us in the face which we can't see at the moment.'

On the following Saturday morning, children were playing on the swings in Blade Park, when one of the children started screaming, 'There's a man lying face down in the bushes!'

One of the parents ran over to look and quickly realised that it was the body of a dead man. He told the children all to move away and go home.

One of the other parents went over to see the body, and then said, 'I will go and fetch the police.'

PC Denstun arrived and informed the two parents that DCI Jackson was on his way from Oakley adding, 'I need you to stay here until he arrives as he will want to speak to you. For now, I need to take your names for future reference about this crime scene.'

DCI Jackson and Bellson arrived together, followed by Tony from forensics. Jackson asked PC Denstun where the body was.

'It's behind the swings in the bushes,' responded PC Denstun.

Jackson and Tony from forensics walked over.

'My God!' shouted Jackson. 'Whoever this is has been murdered in the same way as Sims and Rush were, and there's a crucifix on top of the body again. What the hell does this crucifix mean? Is this some God-fearing person carrying out these murders? Does anybody know who this man is, Denstun?'

'I've seen this person in the village before,' explained PC Denstun, 'but I do not know his name or where he lives. There is a wedding ring on his finger, so I assume he is married.'

'Tony, is there any identification on the body you can see?' asked Bellson.

Tony replied, 'That looks like a wallet in his back pocket.'

Tony removed the wallet and opened it. There was a ten-shilling note and a card with an address on it inside, although there was no name.

Bellson took the card and read the address out and asked Denstun, 'Is this address here in Rislington?'

'Yes, it is; it's a turning off Shipley Lane.'

Jackson spoke to Tony, 'I will leave you to do what's necessary so you can take the body to the forensic lab.'

After that, Jackson left with Bellson to visit the address from the wallet. As they arrived and walked down the pathway to the cottage, the next-door neighbour was out in her front garden. She asked, 'Can I help you? Kim and Brian are away.'

'We are from the police and we need to speak to them. Do you know when they are coming back?'

'Kim went to London a few days ago to visit some friends and should be back tomorrow. I'm not sure about Brian; although I saw him leave the cottage late last night with a small suit case.'

'Thank you for that information, and as soon you see either of them, can you tell them to contact the police as soon as possible as we have some urgent business to discuss with them?'

Jackson and Bellson drove back to Blade Park to see if they could find a suitcase. After searching the area for about thirty minutes, Bellson found a small suitcase hidden in the undergrowth with the name "B. Coots" stamped on the case. 'Sir,' he shouted, 'I've found the case. Its looks like we've found out whose body it is.'

'We can't do anymore until tomorrow when the wife is due to come back from London, so we might as well call it a day, Bellson, and come back tomorrow.'

Mrs Coots arrived at the police station the following day unaware of what had happened to her husband and rang the police doorbell.

PC Denstun answered the door. 'I am Kim Coots. I believe you want to see me.'

PC Denstun responded, 'Yes, we do. Please come in and take a seat. DCI Jackson will come and speak to you in a few minutes.'

'What is going on?' asked Kim anxiously.

'DCI Jackson will explain when he comes to speak to you, Mrs Coots.'

Ten minutes later, DCI Jackson walked into the interview room and introduced himself to Mrs Coots, asking her to prepare herself as he had some bad news for her about her husband.

'What do you mean, about my husband?' asked Kim.

'Mrs Coots, a body was found in Blade Park yesterday morning, and we think it could well be your husband, Brian Coots.'

'It can't be! Brian went to Brighton on Thursday to see some old university friends for a weekend together, so why would he be in Blade Park? Brian would have caught the bus to Oakley from the top of our road to catch a train to Brighton.'

'Mrs Coots, would Brian have a small suitcase with his name on the case?'

'Yes, he would; it is embossed with "B Coots".'

'Well, I'm afraid to say that we found a suitcase near the body we found, and the name 'B Coots' was embossed on the case.'

'This cannot be true,' claimed Mrs Coots, breaking down in tears. She asked, 'Where is this man you believe to be my husband?'

DCI Jackson replied, 'He'll be at the mortuary in Oakley and we will take you there as we need you to identify and confirm that it is your husband. I also have to tell you that this is a murder enquiry.'

An hour later at the mortuary, Mrs Coots tearfully confirmed that the body was that of her husband, Brian. Once she'd calmed down, DCI Jackson took Kim to Oakley Police Station and explained to her that the murder of her husband was identical to two other murders recently in Rislington, and that both victims played for the Rislington cricket club.

'Did Brian play cricket with the club?' asked Jackson.

Kim replied, 'No he didn't. In fact, Brian was not interested in sport at all.'

Jackson asked, 'Would he know Anne Bonn?'

'He may have,' Kim replied, 'as we were all at the same school in Brunton. In fact, Anne and myself were in the same class and we spent a lot of time together. Brian is a year older so I only saw him at school, although I did not know him to speak to. I met Brian in the Hollybush pub three years after I left university. Why are you asking about Anne?'

'The reason I am asking about Anne Bonn,' Jackson explained, 'is that John Sims and Simon Rush, who were also murdered recently, are linked to Anne Bonn through relationships and now your husband has been murdered in the same way as Sims and Rush. There has got to be some link.'

With tears in her eyes, Kim responded, 'What I don't understand is what was Brian doing in Blade Park when he should have been on the bus to Oakley to catch a train?'

'That is what we need to find out, Mrs Coots, but for now, we will get you back home and speak to you when we need to.'

'Can you take me to my daughter's house, as Clare needs to know?'

My colleague, Bellson, will take you and we could do with your daughter's address anyway, as we may need to talk to her at some point. Bellson, take Mrs Coots to see her daughter and I will go and see Anne Bonn to see if there is a connection between her and Brian Coots.'

Jackson arrived at Anne Bonn's house, knocked on the front door which Anne soon opened.'

'I need to come in and speak to you again, Mrs Bonn. I believe you knew Kim Coots at school; her maiden name was Williams.'

'Yes, I did. We were the best of pals at school, but I don't see her these days as we grew apart. Why do want to know that?'

'Well, Mrs Bonn, Kim's husband, Brian, has been murdered, and in the same way as John Sims and Simon Rush.'

'Goodness gracious,' screamed Anne, 'but what has that got to do with me?'

Jackson asked, 'Did you know Brian Coots?'

'Only at school, as I used to see him behind the bike shed for a smoke.'

'What about dating Mr Coots?' asked Jackson.

'Ah, I did go out with Brian a few times. It was nothing serious. I mean, we were only school kids. It was just a bit of fun and as far as I know, nobody else knew. My parents would have killed me if they'd known.'

'So, Mrs Bonn, as far as you know, was this only known by yourself and Mr Coots?'

'Well, yes, and if they did, I don't know who.'

'Mrs Bonn, I have to ask. Are there any other relationships you've had as I need to know before we have any more deaths?'

'I've often flirted with men, but I've not had any other relationships.'

'OK, Mrs Bonn, we will leave it at that for now, but if you can think of anything - no matter how small - about these relationships, then please let me know as soon as possible.'

Back at Oakley Police Station, Jackson walked into his office and found the forensic report on his desk. After reading it, he rang Tony.

'I see that there were green marks and soil on the clothes of the deceased. Does this mean that the body was dragged along the ground?'

'Yes it does. The green is from the grass, and some of the clothes were torn when the body was dragged into the bushes. Being a well-built male, I would say that it had to be a male person who dragged the body and there were no fingerprints so he was obviously wearing gloves again.'

'Thanks for that, Tony.'

Bellson walked into the office and asked if Anne Bonn had dated Brian Coots.

'Yes, she did, but only at school. So where do we go from here? Saying that, it has to be someone who knows Anne Bonn, but who could it be? Is it someone she has rejected and what about these crucifixes? None of them go to church so where the connection of the crucifixes comes in, I can't fathom out. Somewhere in all this paper, there must be a clue staring us in the face, but for the life of me, I cannot see it. It's getting late now, Bellson, so we will call it a day. Let's come in first thing tomorrow morning and go through all the evidence we have.'

Chapter 6

The Final Nail in the Coffin.

Three days later, Felix Mason knocked on the door of Tim Bonn's house.

'Tim, I've come to see if you are available to play cricket this weekend as we have been given the go ahead to use the cricket ground from the police.'

'Yes, I can, but you'd better come in. Although Anne doesn't know it yet, I am going to leave her and get a divorce. I've had enough with what has happened lately, especially with these deaths being linked to Anne. It's all very unsettling. Did you know about John Sims and my wife?'

'To be honest with you, not about John Sims, but there was a rumour going around that Anne was seeing one of the cricket team. However, nobody knew who, and as for John, he would have been the last person I felt could do that to a team-mate.'

'When do you intend to tell Anne?'

'Tonight, when Anne comes home. It's no use putting it off any longer, and then it will be up to Anne as to what she wants to do. We rent this property, and all I shall want is a one-bedroom cottage to live in, as I don't intend to leave the village. Anyway, regarding this Saturday, I will be available to play.'

Later that day, Anne came home and Tim called her into the front room and told her straight, 'Anne, I am fed up with your philandering and you have caused the deaths of three men in your life, so I am going to divorce you.'

'What?' shouted Anne. 'It's not my fault these men have been murdered and you will not divorce me. We are married for life!'

'Well, if that is what you think, you are very much mistaken, Anne. You can pack your bags right now and move out. I don't want anything more to do with you.'

Anne shouted even louder, 'I am not leaving! If anybody is leaving, then it's you!'

Tim shouted back, 'If you think I am going to pay for the rent on this cottage while you stay here, there is no chance of that. I'm fed up of paying for your cosy lifestyle; I buy you expensive clothes, make-up, take you out every Sunday for a slap-up meal and what do you do? You see men behind my back! What do you expect?'

'Anne screamed, 'You are never home during the week and I am here all by myself!'

'Anne, you know damn well that the job I have got takes me all over the country, and it pays me a very high salary. What do think pays for all the luxury items and the lifestyle you lead, which is now finished, by the way?'

'No way!' shouted Anne, after which she started throwing china ornaments around the room, 'You will pay for it. I will kill you before you divorce me.'

'You will kill me?' shouted Tim. 'I could throttle you right now, you little bitch! You have made me look like a fool in front of all my friends in Rislington, so pack your bags and leave right now. In fact, I am going to the pub and when I come back, I will expect you to have left, and if you want a similar lifestyle to what you have now, you will have to find a job and work for a living, because you are not going to get another penny out of me.'

'What do you mean you're going to the pub? You don't even drink Tim!'

'Well, tonight Anne, I am!'

Tim then walked out of his house and saw the neighbours outside who had heard all the shouting between Anne and him.

'I'm sorry if you heard all the shouting, but I have told Anne that I am divorcing her. I am fed up with all her philandering!'

Tim then walked off to the local pub; as it happens, it was a Tuesday night when a few of the local cricket team regularly went for a drink. As Tim entered the bar, Felix spotted him. 'We don't normally see you in the pub, Tim!'

'That's true, but I've just had a flaming row with Anne, and I have told her that I am divorcing her, so I need a drink.'

Tim walked up to the bar and ordered a double whisky 'straight'.

'Wow!' shouted Felix. 'Are you sure? That's hitting the hard stuff!'

'I don't care, Felix. I need a strong drink after tonight.'

'Come and sit with the rest of us, Tim.'

Already sitting at the table were Paul Way, Tom Butch, Ron Cotter and Ray Peterson. Tim then asked them, 'When did you hear the rumour about Anne seeing one of the members of our cricket team?'

Tom replied that it was the night before John Sims was murdered.

'It was tittle-tattle going around the pub and I found it hard to believe that it was John Sims. I always thought that he had a strong marriage.'

'Well, it's done and dusted now. My marriage is over and what Anne does is up to her, but I am staying in the village. I will tell the estate agents that we are giving up the cottage we have and I will look for a smaller place to live. I think I need another double whisky!'

'Careful Tim, you're not used to drinking!'

'I don't care if I get drunk tonight. I just need to get today out of my system.'

By the end of the evening, Tim was not very coherent and his speech was very slurred, so Paul and Tom took him home and managed to find his front door key, take Tim inside and lay him on the settee, leaving him to sleep it off.

When Tim woke up the following day, Anne was still in the cottage. Tim shouted, 'What are you still doing here? I told you to leave last night!'

Anne replied, 'I know you did, but I am not leaving. This is my home and I am staying put.' 'Really?' said Tim, 'Well, today, I am going to the agents we rent this cottage from to give them notice that we don't require this property anymore and to find a one-bed cottage just for me.'

'You can't do that!' shouted Anne. 'This is my home!'

'It was,' Tim shouted back, 'and I pay the rent, not you. So, if you don't leave and the rent is not paid, then the agents will kick you out, so the way in which you want to leave is up to you.'

After saying that, Tim calmly walked out, leaving Anne in tears.

Four days later, on the day of the cricket match, Tim gathered up his cricket gear and left mid-morning even though the cricket match was not due to start until 2 pm. Anne, who was still living at the cottage, asked why he was leaving so early. 'That's none of your business,' retorted Tim and he walked up the garden path and out of the gate. Later that day, Jane, Anne's next-door neighbour, stepped out into her back garden and saw Anne lying on the ground and shouted over the fence to Anne, 'Are you OK?' However, there was no reply, so Jane shouted again and still there was no reply. Confused, Jane went back into her cottage and told her husband Paul, 'I can see Anne lying on the ground and I can't get any response from her.'

Paul then went out of the front door, walked into Anne's front garden and around the side of the house into Anne's back garden.

'Oh my God!' shouted Paul a few seconds later. 'We need the police, as Anne is dead, with a ligature around her neck, and for some reason, there's also a crucifix lying on her body. I can call the police from Anne's house as they have a phone. Jane, please stay in the house, as I don't want you to see this awful sight.'

Paul rang the police and was told not to touch anything and that they would come over as soon as possible. Ten minutes later, PC Denstun arrived, followed by DCI Jackson, Bellson and Tony from the forensics. Paul explained how they came to find

Anne Bonn's body and that he had used Anne's phone to ring them.

Tony checked out the body, and then informed Jackson that she had been murdered in the same way as Sims, Rush and Coots, although the only difference was that there was a foot mark on the back of Bonn. Jackson asked if they would be able to identify the shoe which caused the mark. 'It's possible,' replied Tony. 'It looks like whoever did this put his or her foot on the body back to hold them down while putting the ligature around the neck.'

Jackson asked Paul, 'Did you hear anything unusual this morning?'

'Not a thing, but four or five days ago, there was an almighty row between Anne and Tim which all the neighbours heard, with both of them threatening to kill each other.'

'Do you know what the argument was about?' asked Jackson.

'Yes, Tim told her that he was going to divorce her,' replied Paul.

'Do you know where Tim Bonn is now?'

'That'll be easy, Paul said. 'It's Saturday, so he will be playing cricket and it is a home game today.'

Jackson asked Tony, 'When will you move the body?'

'Give me an hour or two,' answered Tony, 'and then I will have the body removed to the forensic lab to do further tests.'

Jackson then asked PC Denstun to remain on site while he and Bellson drove to the cricket ground. On arrival, they walked into the ground and asked where Tim Bonn was. One of the team shouted out that Tim was in the pavilion, getting ready to bat as he was next in. Tim walked out of the pavilion and asked, 'Who wants me?'

'It's the police for you, Tim.'

'Now what's up?' asked Tim.

Jackson told him, 'I'm afraid we have some bad news for you about your wife.'

'Really?' said Tim. 'She's bad news all the time at the moment.'

Jackson then told Tim what had happened to Anne.

'What?' shouted Tim. 'My life is turning into a nightmare! I need to sit down to be able to take this in. How did it happen and where?'

Jackson explained, 'Your next-door neighbour found her in your back garden this morning. Now, I understand that you and your wife recently had a row and were threatening to kill each other. Is this true?'

'We did. Are you trying to say that I murdered my wife, because, if you are, you are very much mistaken?'

'Well, Mr Bonn, until we establish the facts, you are a suspect and you need to come with us to the police station. They arrived at Oakley Police Station an hour later and Bonn was taken into the interview room. Thereupon, Jackson cautioned Bonn, 'You do not have to say anything, but it may harm your defence if you do not mention when questioned something which you later rely on in court. Anything you do say may be given in evidence. Do you understand, Mr Bonn?'

'Yes, I do,' replied Tim.

'Mr Bonn, I need to know your movements from when you got up this morning and I mean every detail.'

Tim recounted, 'I got up at about 8.30 am, washed and dressed, then made my own breakfast at around 9 am, then washed up the breakfast things. After that, I got all my cricket gear together and left home at 10 am.'

Jackson asked, 'Why did you leave so early when the cricket match didn't start until the afternoon?'

Tim replied, 'I had no intention of coming back home because I was going to look at some properties to rent as I am giving up the property I now live in, as I am going to divorce my wife or should I say now that I was going to divorce my wife?'

Jackson asked, 'Can you prove that you looked at some properties?'

'Yes, I can. I was accompanied by Mr Tisdale from Tisdale agents, from whom I shall be renting. In fact, the cottage I live in at the moment is rented through them. If you don't believe me, then check with them.'

'What time did you finish the viewing?'

'I think it was around midday.'

'Then what did you do?' asked Jackson.

Tim replied, 'I am not answering any more questions until I have a solicitor with me, as this getting ridiculous.'

'We can arrange that. Who is your solicitor, Mr Bonn?'

'It's Tisdale from the letting agency. He's the brother of the person who runs the letting side of the business.'

Jackson told Bellson, 'Ring the solicitor and get him here as soon as possible.'

Thirty minutes later, Jack Tisdale arrived and was told what had happened so far and his reaction was abrupt. 'I should have been called before, especially as Mr Bonn has now been cautioned,' he said.

Tisdale asked, 'What evidence do you have on my client?'

'None,' answered Jackson, 'as we are trying to establish the facts. Now, we need to know what Bonn did between midday and arriving at the cricket ground.'

'Before my client answers that question, I need to speak to him privately,' Tisdale insisted.

Jackson and Bellson left the room and Tisdale asked Tim, 'Do you have an alibi between 12 noon and 2 pm?'

'Not really, as I went for a walk and sat down in Blade Park and there wasn't anybody around. I then got in my car and drove to the cricket ground.'

'That's fine, Tim. You can tell them that and no more.'

Jackson and Bellson were called back into the room and Bonn told them exactly what he had told Tisdale.

'Now, are you going to charge my client? If not, then he is free to go.'

'At the moment, we are not, but I require your client's shoes.'

'What on earth for?' demanded Tisdale.

'It's because there was a foot mark on the back of Anne Bonn where she was held down.' Tisdale reacted, 'Do you mean to say that my client has gone through all this when if you had checked this before and Tim Bonn's shoe had not matched, he'd have been free to go? Why did you not do this first of all? If it does not fit the shoe size, I will expect a full apology from you. This is an appalling way to conduct a murder enquiry.'

Tisdale advised Bonn to give them the shoes they wanted and continued to say that the two of them would go back to Rislington. Tisdale and Bonn left.

'That didn't go very well, did it, Bellson?'
'No sir, and if these shoes are the wrong size, where does that leave us?'
'Somehow, I thought that we had found the missing link at last,' moaned Jackson. 'It's late now and the forensics will be closed, so I will drop these shoes in first thing on Monday morning.'

Chapter 7

The Missing Link

On Monday morning in the Forensic Laboratory, DCI Jackson gave Tim Bonn's shoes to Tony to see if the soles would match the marks on the back of Anne Bonn. 'How long will you need the shoes, Tony?'

'Wait here and you can have them back in about ten minutes.'

After a short while, Tony came back with the shoes, and explained to Jackson, 'They are a similar match, but I cannot guarantee that they are the same shoes, I'm afraid.'

'That's not much help,' replied Jackson.

'Sorry about that, but what I can tell you is that the time of death was between 10 am to midday.'

'Really? That information puts Tim Bonn in the clear as he has an alibi which puts me back at square one.'

'I do have some more information for you about the ligature, Dave.'

'Which is?' asked Jackson.

'The rope is the same as those that boy scout leaders tie around their necks.'

'That's interesting, Tony. Do know if there is a scout troop in Rislington?'

'To be honest, I don't. You would need to ask somebody local like the vicar as scouts are normally attached to the church.'

'Thanks, Tony.'

Jackson picked up Bellson and they drove to the Rislington rectory to see the vicar. As they arrived, the vicar was walking towards the church. Jackson got out of his car and asked if there was a scout troop in Rislington.

'There isn't; the nearest troop is in Brunton, the next village.'

Jackson got back into the car, 'Well, Bellson, we need to go to Brunton as there is a scout troop in that village.'

'That's interesting,' said Bellson, 'because all three of our male victims came from Brunton, and so did Anne Bonn, who was then known as Anne Taylor, and they all went to the same school. Again, the vicar would be our best place to start, I think.'

So, Jackson drove to Brunton. After they had arrived, Jackson asked Bellson if he had any idea where the church was.

'Yes, it's by the green. We passed it when we went to the Hollybush pub, if you remember, and there are four cottages next to the church and the rectory. I think the church is called "Saint Johns".'

Jackson and Bellson arrived at the rectory and knocked on the door. About five minutes later, the vicar opened the door.

'Sorry to bother you, vicar. I am DCI Jackson and this is Bellson. Can we come in and talk to you, please? It is very important.'

"Come in to my office," answered the vicar. "How can I help you?"

'I presume you've heard about the murders that have been happening in Rislington.'

'Yes, I have,' replied the vicar. 'It's an awful business, but what has that got to do with me?'

'I believe you have a local scout troop attached to your church.'

'We do, replied the vicar, 'but as far as being attached to the church is concerned, I don't have a lot to do with them. Anyway, why do you need to know this?'

'The reason I am asking, said Jackson, 'is because all four deaths were caused by strangulation with a lanyard around the neck and we realise now that the lanyard is used by scouts. Also, a silver crucifix has been left with all four bodies. We've already asked the vicar in Rislington about the crucifixes and he has never seen them before. He said that the only crucifix they use is on Palm Sunday, and that is only made from palm leaves.'

The vicar replied, 'I can't help you with the ligatures, but we have some metal crucifixes in the church which we use for Sunday school. Do you have one with you I can look at?'

'I do,' replied Jackson and took one out of his pocket.

'That does look very similar to the crosses we have which we keep in a box in the vestry. I can fetch the box, if you want.'

'Yes vicar, please do.'

Ten minutes later, the vicar brought the box to the church entrance and opened it.

'Look,' said Bellson, 'they're identical.'

'Who would have access to these?' asked Jackson.

'Other than myself, that would only be June, as she used them around Easter time. However, she is quite ill at the moment, so her son also helped her last month, although he lives in Rislington.'

'What's her son's name?'

'His name is Josh. He usually comes over on Saturday nights and stays with his mum, as Josh isn't married.'

Bellson asked, 'What is his last name? It wouldn't be Parry, by any chance?'

'Yes, it is,' replied the vicar.

'Well, I'll be damned,' said Jackson. 'Sorry vicar, I didn't mean to swear. It's been staring us in the face all this time. Where does his mother live, vicar?'

'His mother lives in one of the cottages next to the church, at number two on the green.' 'Right, Bellson, we can walk there. Let's go!'

'Can I come with you?' asked the vicar, 'June is not very well and is getting rather frail.'

'Yes, that would be very helpful, vicar. I will take the box of crucifixes, if that's OK. I'll give them back to you once we have finished our investigation.'

'That's no problem; you can take them.'

'Bellson, put the box in the car, and then we can go and visit Mrs Parry. Vicar, can you knock on the door and introduce us, please, as I don't want to frighten Mrs Parry. Just say that we need to talk to her about Josh.'

As the vicar opened the front gate when they arrived, Mrs Parry was looking out of her front window. The vicar pointed to the front door, asking June to open it for them. Once June had opened the door, the vicar introduced DCI Jackson and Bellson.

'June, they need to ask you some questions about Josh, so can we come in?'

June took them into her front room and asked them to sit down.

'What do you want to know?' she asked.

'Mrs Parry,' began Jackson, 'I gather Josh has helped you out at Sunday school.'

My son has helped me for many years with Sunday school, but not as a teacher, more as an assistant. Whatever I needed doing, Josh would do for me. Why do you ask?'

'Mrs Parry, we want to know about the crucifixes you use on Palm Sunday. Does Josh have anything to do with them?'

'Do you mean the crucifixes we keep in the vestry?' asked June.

'Yes, Mrs Parry.'

'Yes, he does. Josh hands them out to the children and when they're no longer needed, Josh collects them and puts them back in the vestry.'

'Mrs Parry, is your son in the scouts these days?'

'No, not for a long time. He was when he was a teenager, but stopped with the scouts when he was about fourteen years old. He didn't get on very well with some of the other scouts. It was something about some girl in the village. Don't ask me what happened, as I don't know, but for some reason, he has always kept his scout uniform which is up in his room.'

'So, do you mean Josh still uses his bedroom from when he lived here, Mrs Parry?'

'Yes, replied June, 'Josh quite often stays here overnight, although I can't go in his room as he keeps it locked. He tells me not to go into his bedroom.'

'Mrs Parry, we need to look in his bedroom. Where does Josh keep the key?'

'The key is on top of the Welsh dresser in the kitchen which is far too high for me to reach.' Jackson told Bellson to go and find the key. Bellson came back with two keys, and said, 'Sir, I have found a large key and a small key.'

'I presume the small key is for Josh's bedroom, is it Mrs Parry?' asked Jackson.

'Yes, I think so,' she answered.

'Can I see the large key?' asked the vicar. 'I think that's the spare key to the church vestry.' 'Really?' Jackson shouted loudly. 'Did you know that your son had the vestry key, Mrs Parry?'

'No, I didn't. I can't understand why he had the vestry key. What is going on and what has my son done?'

Jackson explained about the murders that had been happening in Rislington, and that Anne Bonn was central to why these murders had happened.

'Your son is now linked, and each victim had a crucifix left on top of them identical to the crucifixes you use on a Sunday.'

'Oh, my goodness me,' cried June, 'what has my son gone and done? What happens now?' she asked.

'Mrs Parry, we need to check your son's bedroom. Bellson, go and unlock the bedroom.'

Bellson went upstairs, and two minutes later, shouted from the bedroom, 'Sir, you'd better come and look!'

Jackson went straight upstairs to the smaller bedroom and Bellson told him to look at the walls of the bedroom.

'Oh my goodness me!'

Every wall was covered in newspaper articles from the local Gazette about different murders that had happened in the past.

'Look, they are all to do with scandals involving illicit affairs.'

'Sir, look over here. There are articles about the murders of Sims, Rush, Coots and Bonn. Its looks to me, Sir, as if he has been studying other killings before he's embarked on his own killing spree.'

'We need to search all the drawers and wardrobes, Bellson,' advised Jackson.

While they were searching, Jackson said, 'Look what I've found: the same lanyards identical to the ligatures around all of our victims' necks with a long tubular piece of leather and some smaller pieces cut to length, which is what was slid over the lanyards when they were pulled tight around the necks of our victims.

'Look, sir. There's an exercise book in this drawer and, oh my goodness, look what's written inside:

"They shall all die for excommunicating me from their circle and Anne Taylor should be my wife. You will all die, and none of you deserve to live. Death to you all!"

I think that's evidence for you, sir!'

'Bellson, all we need now is the instrument which was used to try and knock out each of our victims.'

'Sir, here in the wardrobe is something round wrapped in newspaper. Well, well, well, it's a rounders bat with a pair of black gloves.'

'OK Bellson, take all of the newspaper clippings down. We will take every bit of evidence away with us, then we'll lock the door again, as I don't want anybody else in this room until our investigation is over and Josh Parry has been charged with these murders.

Jackson and Bellson went back downstairs and informed June Parry and the vicar what they had found. June Parry broke down in tears, saying, 'Why would my son do this? He has always been such a good boy to me. It seems that I don't know my own son!'

Jackson told June, 'We have to go now to find your son. Vicar, will you ensure that Mrs Parry will be OK? By the way, Mrs Parry, we have relocked your son's bedroom door and we will keep the key for now. Oh, and vicar, we will also need to keep this vestry key as well. You can have it back once we have finished our investigation.'

After that, Jackson and Bellson drove back to Josh Parry's shoe shop. Just as they arrived, a member of staff was closing the shop and, as DCI Jackson was about to walk over, the member of staff told Jackson, 'We are closed, so you will have to come back tomorrow.'

Jackson explained that he was from the police and needed to see the shop owner right away. He also asked for the staff member's name.

'I am Michael Wilson.'

'Mr Wilson, where is the owner?'

'Josh is in the office at the back of the shop as he is about to pay us our wages.'

Jackson walked to the office and opened the door.

Parry asked, 'Who are you?'

DCI Jackson explained who he was.

'What do want?' asked Josh.

Jackson told Parry to pay his staff and then send them home so that they could talk.

Josh dealt with his two staff members.

'Right, Mr Parry, I have just come from your mother's house.'

'Why have you been to my mum's house? Is she OK? What's wrong with my mum?' shouted Josh.

'Your mum is fine, Mr Parry,' replied Jackson. 'Well, I say fine, but she is very upset after what we found upstairs,' he added.

'What do you mean by that, and why were you upstairs in the first place?'

'Mr Parry, we have been in your bedroom, which you still use, apparently, when you sleep at your mum's house.'

'I keep my bedroom locked; that is my private room and nobody is allowed in my room and you don't have a key for my room.'

'Mr Parry, your mother told us where you keep the key; it was on top of the Welsh dresser in the kitchen.'

Josh shouted, 'My mum had no right to tell you that.'

'Mr Parry, we are the police and we have every right to go where we want and I am now arresting you on the suspicion of the murders of John Sims, Simon Rush, Brian Coots and Anne Bonn. You do not have to say anything, but it may harm your defence if you do not mention when questioned something which you later rely on in court. Anything you say may be given in evidence. Do you understand?'

'Yes, I understand, but you have got the wrong person.'

'Mr Parry, I have all the evidence I need. Bellson, has the police van arrived?'

'It has,' replied Bellson.

'OK, Bellson, take Mr Parry away and I will meet you at Oakley Police Station.'

Jackson locked the shop and drove back to Oakley Police Station. Meanwhile, Parry was placed in the cells, still protesting his innocence. Jackson arrived at the police station, walked into his office to collate the evidence before talking to Parry. Bellson joined Jackson.

'The evidence is overwhelming against Parry, Sir, but he is down in the cells claiming he is innocent.

Jackson replied, 'He can claim whatever he likes, but I know he is guilty, and we have all this evidence from his mum's cottage.'

'True sir. Are you ready to interview Parry now?

'Yes, I am. Get the duty sergeant to bring Parry to the interview room. Do we have a solicitor for Parry and has he spoken to Parry?'

'We do, and he is in the interview room waiting for us,' responded Bellson.

Parry was brought up from the cells to the interview room.

DCI Jackson and Bellson were already there with PC Sue Brittan, who was going to take notes from the interview.

Jackson started, 'I am convening this interview with Josh Parry at 7 pm on Friday the 19th of September, 1933 about the murders of John Sims, Simon Rush, Brian Coots and Anne Bonn.'

'Where's the evidence?' shouted Parry.

'Oh, I have got plenty of evidence,' replied Jackson. 'Let's go back many years to when you were in the scouts. Do you remember that, Mr Parry, and why you left the scouts at around the age of fourteen years old?'

'So I left the scouts. What's that got to do with anything now?'

'I'll ask the questions, not you, Parry. Was it not to do with a girl and some of the other scouts you did not want to know? Was it that girl, Anne Taylor, who later married and became Anne Bonn? Well, was it?' shouted Jackson.

'I can't remember.'

'You mean you will not remember. I don't believe that. Do I have to drag your mother in to get the truth out of you?'

'OK, OK, yes it was, but I don't see what all this has do with what you're accusing me of now.'

74

'Oh, I think it has a lot to do with this case.'

'Why?'

'...because those scouts and the girl are now lying in a mortuary here in Oakley!'

'That doesn't mean that I murdered them.'

'Then explain all the newspaper cuttings from the local Gazette about various past murders about scandals involving illicit affairs, and the murders of Sims, Rush, Coots and Bonn plastered all over your bedroom walls in a locked room that nobody else could see.'

'So, I take an interest in local happenings; that's not a crime, is it?'

'OK Parry, if that's the way you want to play it, explain how each victim had a crucifix left on top of their body which was identical to the crucifixes that you and your mother use at Sunday school at Easter. I know you had the spare key to the vestry as it was found in your mum's kitchen on top of the Welsh dresser.'

Jackson threw the key on to the table.

'Well, explain!'

Parry's face turned very pale and he sat in silence, then started mumbling to himself.

'Stop mumbling!' shouted Jackson.

Parry then said, 'That's nothing to do with me. I don't know anything about these crucifixes.'

'Oh, come on Parry, nobody else used them except for you and your mother and it was you who gave them out and collected the crucifixes from the Sunday school. I know I'm right there.'

'Well yes,' answered Parry, 'but that doesn't prove anything.'

'Oh, I think it will, Parry,' said Jackson as he placed the two lanyards he found in the cupboard drawer with the tube of leather and the pieces of leather tube cut to length in front of a frightened Josh.

'Now explain this. It was found in your room, and again, it is identical to the ligature found around the neck of each of the victims.'

Parry looked at his solicitor who whispered in his ear. Parry then said, 'No comment.'

'What do you mean, "No comment"?' asked Jackson.

The solicitor explained, 'I told my client to say that.'

'Really?' asked Jackson, 'If you think that helps your client, then you are very much mistaken!'

At that point, Jackson put the exercise book and the rounders bat on the table.

Parry shouted in a very loud voice, 'Where did you get that book?'

'We found it in your bedroom, Parry, and look at what is written inside of it. It says "They shall all die for excommunicating me from their circle and Anne Taylor should be my wife. You will all die, and none of you deserve to live. Death to you all!" This was followed by the names of Sims, Rush, Coots and Bonn, and to cap it all, we have this rounders bat wrapped in a newspaper which was in the bottom of your wardrobe and this was used each time you murdered your victim. How do you explain that, Parry?'

Parry sat in silence with his head lowered, then banged the table with his fist, stood up and banged the table again. Jackson told Parry to sit down, then Parry shouted aloud, 'I loved that woman from the first day I met her and all she did was reject me time after time and everybody laughed at me, and she would flirt with every man she could right in front of me, just to humiliate me. She would flaunt herself with every man possible. She would have sex behind the bike shed at school with that Coots guy and Rush, and then even when she was married, I still got to see her with John Sims at the Hollybush pub kissing and cuddling in the snug room at the back of the pub, and she was a married woman! I hated them all and they deserved to die. Yes, I murdered every one of them; death to every adulterous person in the world! God does not approve and they shall all die by the cross and the sword.'

Jackson and Bellson looked at each other, and after listening to that outburst, they were lost for words with that confession, and even the solicitor looked stunned.

'I shall need you to sign the confession, Mr Parry. PC Brittan has written down everything you have said. Do you understand?'

'I do,' replied Parry, 'What happens now?'

'Well, Mr Parry, you will be taken down to the cells and, within the next few days, you will be taken to court. Bellson, get the duty sergeant to take Mr Parry away.'

Parry was taken down to the cells. Bellson looked at Jackson and said, 'I didn't see a confession coming like that from Parry.'

'Nor did I, but least we got our man. Now, we just need the court verdict on what sentence Parry will get.'

Two months later, Parry was found guilty in court of four counts of murder and was sentenced to life imprisonment. As Jackson and Bellson walked out of the courtroom, Bellson looked at Jackson and said, 'It's simply not just cricket.'

'Oh, that's very good Bellson! I like that, *simply not just cricket.*'

The End.

Printed in Great Britain
by Amazon